ROBED TO BE PATIENT AND OBEDIENT AND TO PERSEVERE

INSPIRED BY TRUE EVENTS

WANDA G. ATKINSON

Copyright © 2024 Wanda G. Atkinson.

All rights reserved. No part of this book may be reproduced, stored, or transmitted by any means—whether auditory, graphic, mechanical, or electronic—without written permission of both publisher and author, except in the case of brief excerpts used in critical articles and reviews. Unauthorized reproduction of any part of this work is illegal and is punishable by law.

This is a work of fiction. All of the characters, names, incidents, organizations, and dialogue in this novel are either the products of the author's imagination or are used fictitiously.

ISBN: 979-8-89419-322-9 (sc)
ISBN: 979-8-89419-323-6 (hc)
ISBN: 979-8-89419-324-3 (e)

Because of the dynamic nature of the Internet, any web addresses or links contained in this book may have changed since publication and may no longer be valid. The views expressed in this work are solely those of the author and do not necessarily reflect the views of the publisher, and the publisher hereby disclaims any responsibility for them.

THE EWINGS PUBLISHING

One Galleria Blvd., Suite 1900, Metairie, LA 70001
(504) 702-6708

To a virtuous woman who showed and shared her physical and spiritual strength with those that were assigned to her life and circle.

To a woman who endured by following God and the principles that were instilled in her early life.

To a woman who portrayed and evidenced patience, obedience, and perseverance.

To a woman I'm thankful and honored to call Mother.

CONTENTS

Introduction vii
Robed to Be Obedience, Patience, and Perseverance ix
Characters xi

1	They Always Know 1
2	So Much More 9
3	There's No Need; Press on Your Way 15
4	Love Is 23
5	Where the Master Is 27
6	Viola Reveals a Secret 33
7	What Dad Knew First 37
8	A Moment of Truth 41
9	Moving Forward 51
10	Ma-Ree's Reflection 55
11	More Reflections from Ma-Ree 57
12	Deliverance 61
13	Reflections of Angels 65
14	The Homemaker 67
15	You Are Welcome 71
16	Reflections of a Virtuous Woman 73
17	Counting Blessings One by One 77
18	The Circle of Missing Links 83
19	A New Dimension to Freedom 87

INTRODUCTION

Harmony Johns is a fictitious character. She aspires to become a writer. She has written many pieces but nothing of significance yet. She not only loves to write but also loves storytelling. She has heard many stories in her life, and many of them have inspired her. However, she has held on to one for many years: the story of her mother's life.

Harmony has heard bits and pieces of this story all her life. As she gets older and continues to hear the story, she becomes more intrigued with it. It is timeless, and it has held a special place in her life, mostly for her mother's sake.

At this point, she wants to know the whole story. She doesn't know if it will be possible, but she makes a concerted effort by turning herself into an investigative writer. Even though she knows she is not trained as a reporter, she decides to probe and pull together what she can, based on several factors. She knows she has to rely on several aspects. She has to include her own recollections of hearsay, the information that she gathers from close family members, the main source of the story, and the conclusions that she imagines would equate to the rationale of the story.

Harmony is inquisitive, and she has been blessed with a vivid imagination. She has a strong spiritual connection with her mother. Since she feels deeply about how her mother was treated in the story, she seeks a poetic justification for the accounts and causes of her life.

She knows that her mother is wise but that she has educational limitations; therefore, she tries to complete the missing parts. She listens, meditates, and writes to support the information that she has obtained.

This story contains several fictitious characters. However, it was essential that I provide descriptions to show how the story evolved from many different sources, and to show the uniqueness of each personality, and to prove his or her credibility.

As the story progresses, many questions will be answered. Life proceeds as it was intended to because things will become more distinct. Many elements of the story can be accepted. It is concluded that some things had to occur in order to get to the next level.

After much research and investigating, Harmony begins to get a newer perspective of life: its plan and destiny. She begins to understand that the relationship that she and her mother shared was no coincidence but rather a spiritual bond, which neither understood they had until the journey of this story began.

ROBED TO BE OBEDIENCE, PATIENCE, AND PERSEVERANCE

What Kind of Story Is This?

This is a story of destiny. On this path, there will be many challenges and struggles as people face their fears of the unknown.

It is a story of exploitation and manipulation. Its effects will last a lifetime.

It is a story where the journey requires patience, obedience, and perseverance. Against all odds, it will be imperative to stay focused and be thankful for the smallest things.

It is a story of seeking, finding, and believing in something bigger than oneself. It is a foundation on which one stands. It is a time that will require one to keep a level head, even when one's sanity is questionable.

This is also a story where knowing something about God is a prerequisite. It is important because at this point, the lost need refuge, guidance, and truth. Letting go and letting God will be the answer to delving into the unknown.

This is a story about family, love, secrets, and devotion. Principles, expectations, and simplicity will be the basis for structured family life.

It is a story of the fulfillment and delighting in doing small things to make a difference in someone else's life. It's also a story about being able to understand other people's feelings and ways of life and standing in the gap to fill voids that otherwise will not be filled.

This story is also about embracing friendships. Special bonds and lifelong friendships will be the factors that help develop and sustain character with sensitivity through the good and bad times.

This story is finally about trusting in God and His wisdom to live and complete the life He has given. It will take the main source of the story, characters' nuances, and even the twists and turns all working together to provide the description of this story and to fulfill its destined plan.

CHARACTERS

Hessa Murcel Johns (called Destine), who is the mother, is a beautiful brown-complexioned woman. She has long beautiful hair. She's nicely built. She is wise but sad much of the time. She is a Christian, who believes in God and His ways. She believes in and loves family at all costs. She's caring and sharing.

Thaddeus Johns (called Thad), who is the father, is a handsome medium-brown-complexioned man who is incredibly wise. He too has nice hair. He's loving and kind. He is protective of his wife and family. He's a hard worker. He's a good mediator. He believes in good family values.

Neva Johns Stoner (called Aunt Neva) is a medium-height, slender woman. Her skin is fair and exceptionally smooth. She's good-natured. She is a people person who is adored for her kindness. She forever displays her Christian values.

Simon Stoner (called Uncle Simon) is a very short, bald, and heavyset man. He has a dark brown complexion. He is very stern and firm. He has many Christian values, but he doesn't play when it comes to serious family matters. He knows how to handle his business.

Bernie Lee Stoner (called Bernie Lee) is of a medium height, and he has a dark complexion. He is good-natured. He is a jokester. He is informative.

Marie Johns Wadley (called Ma-Ree) is of a medium height. She is dark. She is a people person, and she has a serious nature. She's firm but fair. She loves her family members and protects them.

Mark Murcel is a short stout dark-brown-complexioned man. He always looks angry. He is evil, manipulative, and controlling. He doesn't seem to like people or himself. He doesn't seem to know how to relate to people. He doesn't seem to be rational.

Hazel Murcel is a short woman of medium build. She has extremely long shiny hair. She's nervous and edgy. She wants to do what's right but has no confidence in herself; therefore, she takes abuse and chooses it as a lifestyle.

Viola Murcel Blackmore is also a beautiful brown woman. She is feisty, courageous, unafraid, and unapologetic.

Mark Jr. Murcel (called June Boy) is short and of a dark complexion. He is unsteady and somewhat unstable.

Irene Blackmore is a medium-brown-complexioned woman. She is the daughter of Viola Blackmore, who recalls information from her mother.

Cedelia Eddie (called Cede) is a busybody. She spreads gossip. She is a very tall heavyset woman. She has fair skin and talks with a long drawl.

Elizabeth Johns Brinson is a tall woman. She is dark-complexioned. She appears to be privileged and snooty.

Sahana P. Brinson (called Patience) is a beautiful brown-complexioned woman. She has long silky hair. She appears to be uppity. She is well educated.

Maddie Thornier is white. She appears to be nice and caring. She seems to be a woman of faith who knows some of the story.

Harmony Johns is the narrator, researcher, and author of the events in this story. She is a daughter who is connected to her mother because they shared like energy. The mother has a story to tell but can't write. It becomes so intriguing to the daughter that she feels she is a deeper part of it. This makes her interpret and define the story from a poetic perspective.

Talbot Johns (Tab) is a tall, fair-skinned, and handsome man. He is one of Hessa Johns sons. He too remembers information concerning mother.

1

THEY ALWAYS KNOW

Someone always appears to know something about every aspect of life. Sometimes that person's information is true, sometimes it's made up of rumors, but most of the time, it's pure gossip. These types of people are always unsteady. They complete your sentences. They have to say the last word in a dialogue. They are competitive when it comes to knowing something. They also hear other people's conversations. If they like what they hear, they steal the story, and it becomes part of their archive.

Miss Cede was that type of person. She swore with absolute certainty that what she was telling was the truth. She spoke without hesitation. She spoke as if what she was saying was nothing but factual. She was an acquaintance of our family. She was a very tall, heavyset woman. She had fair skin, and she spoke with a long drawl. Her drawl alone could hold your attention. In my mind, it's what made her conversations so interesting. It was obvious that she used her creativity while telling her stories.

I can recall Miss Cede visiting our home a few times. She lived in the city while my parents lived in a rural area. I can't recall my parents ever saying that they had visited her.

My parents lived in a large country home in the community known as Bare Bush, which was in Oliveville, North Carolina. They had a large front yard and backyard. Steps led up to our front door. There was also a cozy screened-in front porch.

One day, a car pulled up. My mother asked who was there. I recognized who it was and immediately told her that it was Miss Cede. My mother didn't react. She knew it was going to be a dreadful visit. At least, that was my perception. When Miss Cede got out of her car, I believe that I heard my mother grunt under her breath, but at the same time, she told me to ask her to come in.

We welcomed Miss Cede and made our pleasantries. I went repeatedly from the kitchen to the den, where Mother and Miss Cede were sitting. Mother had been cooking. I watched the food for her so that it would not delay our meal.

I heard them talking about general topics until Miss Cede started sharing a story that her mother had shared with her. Although she wanted to share the story, she wanted to make sure that it was okay with my mother. Before Miss Cede started telling the story, she told my mother that she thought the people were related to her. Mother advised Cede that she couldn't tell her whether they were related unless she continued and told my mom who they were.

At that point, Cede continued but decided that she wasn't going to use names. She said she had lived near a family, which had consisted of a husband, a wife, and three children. She described the man as a short, stout, and angry man. She even implied that it seemed he may have had mental issues. He didn't seem to be very friendly. His wife was short and fair-skinned, and she had long silky hair. She was of medium build, and she seemed scary and nervous.

She further explained that the oldest daughter was a beautiful brown-complexioned girl who seemed to be very friendly. She then mentioned the only boy in the home. She had been told to be careful around him because he wasn't too bright.

Every once in a while, Cede would stop talking and look toward my mother, as if she wanted to see if she could get a reaction out of her. Mother just listened and let Cede talk. Cede's mother had said that there had been another girl in the home. This girl seemed quiet and distant. She was very pretty and, she had long silky hair like her mother. The girl seemed lonely.

Every once in a while, Cede reminded my mother that she was telling the story the way her mother had told it to her. She wanted my mother to understand that.

Cede said she had heard many dark stories about this family. She said that her mother had visited them one day, despite having heard that the man of the house had a mean streak. Her mother hesitated to go because she had heard how abusive he was to his wife and younger daughter.

Cede did say that her mother was nosy and that she wanted to know firsthand what was going on in that house, despite all the speculations and rumors she had heard through the grapevine. Her mother used the fact that they were neighbors as an excuse to meet them.

Her mother only visited the house one time. She was nervous, but she had peeped out of her window and watched the husband leave, so she knew that this was her opportunity. Her mother knocked on the door, and the wife invited her in. She and the wife talked about several things, but the wife had a stutter and seemed nervous and edgy. The wife kept looking around, and it made Cede's mother even more nervous. Her mother and the wife discussed many things, but it was hard for Cede's mother to understand everything because of the woman's speech impediment.

The wife said that she felt joy and pain as she talked about her children. Her husband loved their boy and the oldest girl, but he did not love their youngest girl and treated her badly. At that point, Cede's mother was ready to leave because she didn't know what to say. She didn't respond to it and started talking about something else.

Cede's mother saw all the children. The oldest girl and the little boy seemed carefree and playful. The youngest girl was quiet and lonely. The little boy was mischievous and always doing something where his mother had to get after him. Cede's mother thought that there was an eerie feeling in the house, which led her to think that something was not right.

Cede's mother wanted to leave before the husband got back, but as she got up to go, he entered the house. Her mother's heart started pounding. As she was leaving, she spoke to him, but he only grumbled under his breath. When Cede's mother looked at the wife, she noticed that her attitude had changed. She had become quiet, and she didn't even walk her to the door. Cede did not know if her mother was exaggerating, but she said that when the husband entered the house, a bad spirit came in with him.

Although Mother sat and listened to the story, she decided to change the topic. She told Cede that she had been cooking dinner and asked her if she was planning to join us. Mother never told Cede if she had already known the story or anybody in it.

As Cede had told the story, I could tell that Cede was getting on my mother's nerves. Mother had shown very little emotion as Cede had ranted. It was as if she had been able to endure and dismiss it at the same time.

At any rate, Cede apparently had not realized how long she had been talking. She looked at her watch and decided that she could not stay for dinner. She knew she had a long drive home and decided it was time to go. Cede even apologized for prolonging the conversation. Mother walked Cede to the door. As Cede was driving off, my mother said that Miss Cede talked all the time and that she wouldn't let anyone get a word in.

After Cede left, I followed my mother to the kitchen and asked if she needed my help. Mother said that she had everything under control. After having listened to Miss Cede's story, I had questions for my mother. I first asked Mother the reason that she had seemed disinterested in the story. Next, I asked how well she knew Miss Cede. I also asked her if she knew Cede's mother. I finally asked if Cede was talking about my mother's story. Mother said that it sounded like her story; however, she didn't elaborate. She also said that she knew Cede from church but didn't really Cede's mother. She had been told that Cede and her mother were busybodies and that they kept things stirred up.

Mother deflected attention from them by telling me a story about Cede and her family. It was rumored that Cede's parents dabbled in witchcraft. They both had physical afflictions, and they were very envious of people.

Aunt Neva told Mom that they used to come to her house and irritate everyone there by singing for terribly long periods, especially when they had neighborhood gatherings. They also drank heavily. They acted like a couple of clowns when they sang gospel songs. Cede's father preached, and her mother shouted one minute and then cursed the next.

Mother's Uncle Simon told her how Cede's father had a reputation for putting curses on people. People were careful not to say certain things around the couple because they twisted and turned things around and caused a lot of disturbances in their community.

Mother told me that she liked Cede and that she could deal with her. She tried to be patient with them, especially when so many people were against them. Most people at their church couldn't deal with Cede because she had caused so much confusion and been in people's business.

Mother shifted the conversation again by telling me how thankful she was for my father. She spoke with such joy about how she and my father had stayed together and kept all of us children together. She looked at all of us as gifts. My mother was very passionate when it came to her family. Mother even expressed how much she loved us and that she always wanted the best for us.

I listened to her words very carefully as she spoke about our family. At the same time, I wondered how we had gotten on the subject of family. Some key words stood out and made me realize that she looked at all of us as blessings. She explained that there had been times when she hadn't been able to see how she would raise us, but she had never stopped hoping that she was doing the right thing. She knew that she wasn't going to be a good mother overnight but that if given the time, she would keep trying. Through all our family challenges, she had peace, joy, and fulfilment in her life.

After the day was over, I reflected on Miss Cede's conversation. I also thought about all the things my mother had shared with me. Many thoughts ran through my mind. As I meditated, I took out my pen and notebook and started writing. Two thoughts stood out to me. One was about Miss Cede and her busybody ways. The other was about the sad things Cede had said about the seemingly dysfunctional family.

I began writing a poem called "They Always Know." These words came to mind while trying to describe Miss Cede and her conversation.

THEY ALWAYS KNOW

Have you ever met someone
There is always someone out there
Who seems to know it all?
Your words have no validity.
All the shots, they call.

They know the things of the world,
Religion they also know.
On each, they speak with certainty.
From their mouths, they just let it flow.

You never tell them anything new.
They always say, "I know."
News just seems to fill the air
So they can let it flow.

It's a one-sided conversation
Where you can't get in a word.
When telling people who know everything,
They will always say, "I heard."

They have itchy ears and rolling tongues.
They sit around, and they prey
On words they hear and twist around
So they can have the final say.

The words that Mother had shared in the kitchen were touching to the point that they gave me further words to write.

HE GIVES

He gives us the breath of life
At the moment of our birth.
He chooses those that He will entrust
To welcome us here on Earth.

He gives each of us five senses
That can direct and help us relate
In a world that is full of challenges
So that we can function and operate.

He gives us hope when it seems hopeless.
Because of Him, we can dare to dream
And reach out to all possibilities,
No matter how remote they seem.

He gives us time and infinite endurance.
Like an eagle, He lets us soar
To heights that seem so unreachable,
Taking us where we've never been before.

He gives us peace amid adversities.
He gently calms our every storm.
He covers us with His saving grace.
He keeps us from danger and harm.

He gives us joy and love despite
All the good and bad that we do.
His presence, we may not always feel,
But He's with us. This I know is true.

2

SO MUCH MORE

All the beating around the bush that Cede did on her visit reminded me of the story Aunt Neva had told us about our mother. We heard the same story often, especially when we visited Aunt Neva and Uncle Simon. Mother also told us the story many times.

Even though I had heard it repeatedly, I always felt something had been left out for a reason. Several parts of the story were similar, but I knew there were missing parts. I can't speculate as to whether facts were omitted to spare our feelings or for another reason.

My Aunt Neva was a good woman. She was a medium-complexioned woman. She was slender and nicely built. She was very spry. She was a compassionate person who had an air about her that especially made young children attracted to her. Not only the young people clung to her, but she also had the kind of spirit that ignited love in all people.

Uncle Simon, her husband, was a short, bald, and heavyset man. He was staunch, firm, and serious. Although he had a softer side, he showed his firm side most of the time. Many people didn't know how to take him, and he didn't seem to mind that at all.

Cede's story had sent me into reminiscing mode. I remembered Aunt Neva telling us the story of Mark and Hazel Murcel. They were my mother's (Hessa) parents. Aunt Neva told us that she and Uncle Simon had taken Mother in when she was around twelve years old. She described her as being a pretty girl who was very sad. She said that Mother didn't need to be in Hazel and Mark's home because if she had stayed, she would have never survived.

Aunt Neva said that ever since she had known Mark, he had acted like he had problems. She said he seemed angry all the time. He didn't appear to be friendly; she never saw him laughing or smiling.

She also said that Hazel was a good person, but she got tangled up with the wrong man. Hazel had limitations of her own to cope with. She was a nervous type of person.

Aunt Neva said that it didn't take much to make Mark upset. Every time he would have one of his spells, he would tell our mother that he wasn't her father. He would curse her out and throw anything he could get his hands on to intimidate her. He told our mother how much he hated her and wanted her out of his house.

According to Aunt Neva, Hazel did her best, but she was very fragile herself. She was afraid of Mark. She was brave enough to protect our mom from danger many times, but sometimes, it really got rough.

Hazel was Uncle Simon's biological niece. Uncle Simon didn't really care for Mark, and he was not afraid of him. They butted heads many times. Uncle Simon would go over to Mark's house because someone from the community had informed him that there was screaming and clamor going on at that house. Uncle Simon would go over and confront Mark, and Mark would deny everything.

She remembered Hazel telling them that Mark threw an axe at our mother. It just missed her by a smidgen. Hazel told our mother to run to Neva and Simon's house. After Mother had gotten to their house, she was gasping and afraid. At that point, Aunt Neva and Uncle Simon took her in for good. Mother had nothing but the clothes on her back.

Aunt Neva could tell that Mother was very wise and that she wanted to learn. She had been denied the opportunity because of Mark's hatred toward her. Aunt Neva witnessed Mark telling Mother that he was not going to buy her any books because she was not his child.

When they first took our mom in, she was shaken and was broken inside. She was quiet and distant. Aunt Neva and Uncle Simon provided food, clothing, and shelter. Aunt Neva made her clothes, talked with her, and showed her love. She also gave her hope. After Mother got used to staying with Aunt Neva, she opened up to her. Mom said that she had to travel a path where she would have to learn to be a survivor. Mother had already predicted that she would have a hard life.

Our mother was very obedient to Aunt Neva and Uncle Simon. She was always doing something around the house to earn her keep, even though they didn't require it of her. Aunt Neva saw something in our mother that let her know Mom would be fine. Mother thanked her repeatedly for rescuing her. Aunt Neva often told our mother to be patient and obedient and to persevere so that she would be able to make it in life. She told Mom this as often as she could. She also told her to place those words in her mind and heart.

I felt that I should add something to my journal about how mother must have felt before and after Aunt Neva took her in. I could only imagine, so this is how I perceived it to be for Mother. She wanted so much more for her life. She was silently yelling it out to anyone who would listen.

SO MUCH MORE

Help me! Save me from this life of wretchedness!
Hear me! Feel my cause in this world full of promises.
Help dry my tears and silence the midnight screams
That interrupt my hopes, my beliefs, and my dreams
Of a new life and beginning that can help, my soul redeem.

Spare me from this failing test, which always equals poor.
I know that I am destined to be and to do so much more.
There's no life but only restlessness in this place of suffering and woe.
There's always thoughts of leaving and anxiousness. Help me. I have to go!

There's always an excuse to accuse and abuse little ole me.
In the silence, there are questions, but then I just let it be.
There's no one to stand up for my cause or for righteousness.
There's only someone seeking out the bad and never seeing my best.
There are no utterances of encouragement and comfort or any kind of joy.
But there's always disputing, squabbling, and so much anger to employ.

Nothing is ever exciting here. There's no life here to adore.
That's why I feel that I'm destined to have so much more.
If only someone would believe and show that there is still hope;
Someone who could stand firm and boldly untie this dreaded rope,

Someone who discerns my deepness from the depths of my very soul
And understands a heart's brokenness. This is a story to be told.
Is there *anybody* out there who will come and see about me?
I must believe in your unrest; my faith won't let it be.
With *help*, I believe I will find the key to open this horrid door
And fulfill my dreams and destiny, which offer so much more.

MS. MADDIE THORNIER
(Reflection 1)

Aunt Neva used to live near and worked for Ms. Maddie. Mother worked for her as well when she was a young girl. According to Aunt Neva, Ms. Maddie really cared for Mother.

One day, I visited Ms. Maddie at the request of Aunt Neva. She had told Aunt Neva that she would like to see me. She had not seen me since I was a little girl. I couldn't understand the reason that Ms. Maddie would specifically ask for me. I decided that she might be able to provide some useful insight that would add to my writing mission.

During the visit, Ms. Maddie told me how much I resembled my mother. She told me how smart and kind she was. She told me that my mother was incredibly sad and quiet during the days that she had worked for her. Many times, she would try to get Mother to open up to her because she thought she might be able to help her. She wanted to advise her, but Mother wouldn't share her feelings.

Ms. Maddie always had faith that Mother would have a better life because she was good, kind, and very respectable. She could feel that Mother had the right kind of spirit in her. She had heard how Mother had been treated in her life, and she often prayed for her. She had told Mother many times to hold on and be patient.

3

THERE'S NO NEED; PRESS ON YOUR WAY

One day, I was talking to my brother Talbot (Tab). I brought up the subject of our mother's early life. To my surprise, he reminded me of some things that I never knew he was privy to.

Mother often told us how hard she had worked. The spirit that dwelled in her never allowed her to be slothful or lazy. It didn't matter whether she was working on the farms or doing housework, she gave it 100 percent because she knew that was the right thing to do. She never made much money. Sometimes, she was compensated with hand-me-downs.

Through it all, she gained peace of mind. Through her struggles, God had put songs in her heart. Even before she went to live with Aunt Neva, words poured into her heart to assure her that she was not alone and that she was going to make it through her wilderness.

Tab reminded me of one of the songs, which was called "You're Not Alone." Mother didn't think that she was a singer, but she would give a small rendition of the song. She would quietly sing,

> You're not alone
> You're not alone
> Take your rest my sweet child
> You're not alone.
> You must have faith
> You must believe
> Ask what you will
> You will receive
> I made a promise
> I heard your plea
> You're not alone.

Mother was afraid to get excited about anything. Even when things were getting better for her, she was always afraid. No matter what good thing happened in her life, she tried to remain humble.

As she let this attitude develop, another song came into her heart. She relied on her memory for the words to the song because she didn't write. She described her songs as God-given. That's why she could sing them the way they were given to her. With humbleness, she would sing,

> If I should Glory
> I'd Glory in Jesus
> If I should Glory
> I'd Glory in God.
> He is my Savior

I know He loves me
I'll Glory in Jesus
He'll set me free.

Half the time, Mother did not understand what the songs meant, but she knew they must have been necessary for the path that had been chosen for her.

Tab asked me if I could remember the countless times that Mother had talked about her life's story. It was clear to him that her pain still ran deep. Even though she had continued with her daily life, inwardly, trying to get over what she had been through had been a task.

Tab also told me that he had watched our mother busily doing what she does and then suddenly developing an attitude for no apparent reason. If he asked her about it, she would deny it and resume normalcy. I acknowledged that I too had witnessed this many times, but I knew it was harmless.

While we were on the subject, we both spoke about our mother's tone. We agreed that Mother was a wonderful mother, but while sometimes listening to her tone, it was hard to believe. Many times in general, Mother would sound as if she was fussing. We would ask what the problem was because of her tone. She would always tell us that nothing was wrong. We agreed that we didn't think she was aware of how she sounded at times. But again, we knew it was harmless.

Tab said that we all had felt the effects of what Mother had gone through. Tab provided an example to explain what he meant. Mother wanted one of us to do something. She kept on saying the same thing until she got favorable results.

I shared with Tab how talented our mother was. We all knew this. For example, she was an avid quilter. This was the only thing that could almost make her relax. However, as she quilted, she would start talking about her past. We would listen and sometimes ask questions.

I shared with Tab a couple things that I had noticed Mother doing around the house throughout our lives. She had a few peeves. Mother was fixated on closing drawers at any given time. It aggravated her to no end to see a drawer open in the kitchen or any other room. She was always pressing down a drawer's contents so that it would have a neat appearance. She told us many times of a certain lady named Tessie who kept a sloppy home. Clothing hung out of drawers, making the home look less than neat.

Mom swept the floors often. It irritated her to see even a small piece of trash on the floor. She was steadily picking up even the smallest thing. She liked the kitchen table to be kept neat. After she had cleaned it off, she didn't like us to put something back on the table. She would place things where they were supposed to be.

We agreed that Mother was a strong woman, but she couldn't be still. She kept busy all the time. When she tried to relax, she would sit for a moment and then start twiddling her thumbs. She was antsy.

Mother would start the conversation by telling us that her father hated her. She would tell us how he beat her. She would tell us how he degraded and cursed her in front of others. As her children, we always believed there were parts that Mother deliberately left out¾the parts that were hurting her the most. We agreed that we had to accept the way that Mother told her story on her own terms.

Every once and a while, she would share another part of her story. I remember Mother telling some of us that she never imagined she would be able to have children. She said that she had gone through several miscarriages early on. She attributed them to the beatings that her father gave her in her early years. Tab and I agreed that Mother was probably withholding information. None of us pushed Mother because we knew that she could easily slip into another zone.

Most of us knew when we had said enough about the subject. If her expression changed on us, and sadness appeared, one of us would signal to the others that we should leave the subject alone, even if she had initiated it. I told Tab and he agreed that Mother's story had to be told by her at her own discretion.

Tab asserted that even though Mother's life was hard, she was not a quitter. He thought that her faith in God was what kept her going. I agreed. Many times, Mother had told us that God had brought her that far and that she trusted God to get her through her burdens, pains, and worries. She has told us that no matter how bad it seemed or looked, she would never doubt God. I'm often reminded of what Mother said Aunt Neva told her to put into her heart and mind as a young girl which was to be patient, obedient, and to persevere. Mother always said she kept these words and practiced them daily.

Because Tab and I had had a lengthy discussion, I needed to meditate and reflect on it. Before I retired for the night, I took out my notepad and summarized my thoughts. I concluded that there was no need to let someone else's bad choices define or confine you into a prison (in your own mind) so that you felt there was no escape.

THERE'S NO NEED

No one said it would be easy.
No one said it would be fair.
But I know there is a Savior,
And He keeps us in His care.

No matter how heavy the burden,
No matter how deep the pain,
Keep trusting and believing,
And there will be joy again.

There's no need to keep your worries.
In time, the tears will cease.
It doesn't matter what it looks like,
In Him you can find peace.

There's no doubt you must run on.
Run on and do it with haste.
His promises and your endurances
Will help you win this race.

I keep thinking that if Mother could have forgotten her past completely and moved on, it would have been much better for her. I journaled my thoughts regarding how I wished Mother could keep pressing on and not look back.

PRESS ON YOUR WAY AND DON'T LOOK BACK

Press on your way and don't look back.
Your future is just ahead.
Don't tarry long on the used-tos.
Focus on the *now* instead.

Through all hurts and disappointments
And thoughts of all hope being gone,
Press on your way and look forward
To a future and a different zone.

Many times, you have been rejected.
Personally, you know that it was wrong,
But press on your way and don't look back.
Be resilient, and yes, be very strong.

You've been criticized from every angle.
You've been wounded on every side.
Press on your way and don't look back.
Take these difficulties in stride.

Life's journey is never ever easy,
No matter what you have or lack.
Don't give up and keep on moving,
By pressing and not looking back.

4

LOVE IS

It's amazing that in the many times that Mother had told us her story, the details had taken on new meanings. Most of my life, I had only listened to Mother, but suddenly, I really heard what she was saying.

Mother was a serious-minded woman, and even though she was content with her life, she didn't smile a lot. There is a saying that opposites attract, and in the case of she and our father, this was true. Our dad, Thaddeus (called Tad), was very strong physically and emotionally. He was also a jokester. He took life seriously but not so much that he couldn't enjoy it. He smiled often, and he was pleasant most of the time.

Mother's way of dealing with us children was to do everything in a politically correct way. On the other hand, our dad required us to do as we were told, but he would not judge it as a serious issue unless he saw that it would cause confusion between him and our mother. He and Mother were mostly on the same page when it came to us children.

I remember Mother explaining how she had met our dad. Several people told her that Daddy had been watching her for years and that he thought she was very pretty. Some of their acquaintances were against their relationship because of their age differences. Dad was six years her senior. She was in her early teens when our dad first noticed her.

As she continued with her explanation, she gave us a description of herself in her earlier years. She said she had long, beautiful hair. She had a beautiful figure, and many people told her so. She always presented herself naturally. She never liked lipstick or any kind of makeup.

Mother always told us how blessed she felt when Daddy had come into her life. She called him her best friend. She had known instantly that their love was meant to be. Mother described our dad as being handsome. Other women had their eyes on him, but she knew in her heart that she and Daddy were meant for each other. She really didn't worry about the other women.

I remember how Mother lit up when she spoke about Dad and their relationship. She said that once they got married, her life started taking shape, and she began to feel some self-worth. She knew that she had found true love. She began to understand many things. They did everything together. Early on, she learned the concept give-and-take. His very presence gave her real hope and a real chance. She could finally breathe freely.

As Mother spoke about the love of her life, I could imagine all kinds of romantic situations. Her love story was simple but perpetual. Mother would praise God by saying, "What a friend we have in Jesus for sending me a best friend." She and my dad became friends first. Dad had many issues. Although he was an only child, he was reared by aunts and uncles.

As my mom and dad's love grew, they got married. She'd often say that they climbed Jacob's ladder together. She knew she had found her soul mate and that she was in it for a lifetime according to the vows that she believed and received.

Mother explained that she had almost been afraid to be so happy. She always tried to keep a sober mind and remember how she had gotten that far. She knew it had been God. She knew that even though she was very happy, she still had to be patient, remain obedient, and continue to persevere.

We listened attentively as Mother shared a portion of their love story. I remember us watching Dad as our mother told it and the way it made him blush. He shook his head and shyly smiled as Mother spoke about her love and admiration for him. It shocked us when Mother talked so freely about her love for Dad. She told us about the relationship, but she didn't give us personal or private details because she didn't talk that way around us.

Since this was a good memory, I decided to journal about this love story. I wanted to express what love was and to share what Mother said and didn't say.

LOVE IS

Love is like a ship sailing on waves that impress the sea.
Love is finding heart's destination where it was meant to be.
Love is gentle as the morning's dew, which falls upon the grass.
Love is endless and timeless; the roots just last and last.

Love is as real and genuine as the name given you at birth.
Love is a strong emotion, which is regarded on this earth.
Love is an expressive action to be received and understood.
Love endures the test of time, whether dire or whether good.

Love is a match for a couple, who fulfills their roles' intent.
Love is open communication without commands twisted or bent.
Love is likened to a distribution shared wholly and unselfishly.
Love is an emotional appeal, desired with a touch of honesty.

Love is people, places, affection, and an array of other themes.
Love is hope for the future, fulfilling impossible dreams.
Love is praying for one another in a world of many mysteries.
Love is helping the hungry and thirsty souls fulfill their destinies.

Love is delivering and transmitting feelings that are so inescapable.
Love is necessary, easily caught, and contagious, making anyone capable.
Love is patient and needing of attention and participation
From an open heart and a focused mind for an everlasting relation.

5

WHERE THE MASTER IS

Aunt Neva was our father's biological aunt. They were very close. Dad's mother was Aunt Neva's sister. She only had one son, who was named Bernie Lee. Bernie was a jokester, but whenever he talked about our mother, he was serious and very compassionate.

While she lived with them, the two of them became very close. Bernie told us that our mother, Hessa (called Destine), had often talked about the many battles that had trailed her. She said that she knew she was a good person and that she wanted to do the right thing in life. Bernie confirmed that these facts were true. No matter what happened, her brokenness seemed to haunt her every day. She couldn't seem to escape it. Her scars were deep.

Bernie said that Mother had had many fears when she had moved in with them. She had been raised in a house full of superstitious people (even her mother). Her mind was on ghosts, witchcraft, and superstition; things she always heard her family talk about.

Bernie told us a story that our mother's father had told her, which had instilled more fear in her life. He made her fear doves. Her father often threatened her by saying that if she went outside and heard a dove coo, she would certainly die. She became so shook up after hearing a dove, Aunt Neva had to explain that it was just a bird.

Mother would get up early in the morning and pace in each room as she tried to tune out the sound of a dove. She would cry out and express how sad she thought the bird sounded. She lost a lot of sleep because she believed that the sound of the dove meant she would die.

Uncle Simon had even chimed in and explained that a dove was a peaceful creature and nothing to be afraid of. Bernie said that his dad was a Christian and knew the significance of the dove. Bernie recalled his dad telling our mother that even though the dove sounded like it was bringing sadness, it was doing the opposite. The dove represented love and peace.

WHY DO DOVES COO?

Why do you coo outside my window,
By my window at the crack of dawn?
I toss and turn. My rest, I break
'Cause your cooing goes on and on.

I distance myself, going from room to room.
The echoes follow me so lonesomely.
What is it? What do you want?
Your cooing is frightening me.

I don't understand the language of the coo,
So how do we communicate?
Your cooing seems to keep chasing me.
I want to know soon and not late.

I felt the craze as I spoke out loud.
I felt my sanity was being attacked
When I talked to a dove at the crack of dawn.
God help me for the sense I've lacked.

I prayed and searched for answers.
I prayed and did not cease.
I asked why doves kept cooing.
The answer was, *To bring you peace.*

Peace for what? Peace for what?
I'm fine, but I don't understand.
From the burdens I have borne from this old world,
Perfect peace is all over the land.

'Cause when your burdens are heavy,
And that truly is the case,
The cooing delivered by the dove
Ascends from a heavenly place.

Don't be afraid of the dove's, "Coo, coo."
It didn't come to frighten you.
It just obeyed a great command.
Understand and God bless you!

Bernie said that he had never been a frightened person but that our mother made him nervous because of the things she had gone through. He would hear Aunt Neva and Uncle Simon saying that Mark had really tortured that child. Even though he didn't hear them say it, he knew that it had been rough on Mother before she came to live with them.

On her best good day, she would tell him that the battle going on in her mind was too big for her. She knew that she needed to turn it over to God, but she was having a hard time doing so.

Because Bernie and our mother had grown up together, they stayed in constant contact. After she had accepted Christ, he saw some changes in her demeanor. Mother was devoted to the church and her church family. He was very excited that she had gotten involved and that she could try to move forward.

She was excited about the people she had met through organizations she had joined. She joined a woman's club, which gave her a chance to hear other women's stories about their lives. Mother enjoyed people and fellowshipping. Even with this, she knew that she had to be patient and obedient and to persevere.

Our whole family loved Cousin Bernie. He wanted to tell us things about our mother so that we would understand her better. He told us not to repeat what he had said because he wanted to keep the peace with our mother. She trusted him.

Bernie said that when she first moved in with them, our mother was very quiet and reserved in the house. At first, she even broke his heart because she wouldn't laugh at his jokes, which made him think that he was losing his touch. Many times, he caught her crying. Sometimes he would console her, and sometimes he would just let her cry it out. Aunt Neva would sometimes go into her room and talk with her. Aunt Neva would hold her and remind her that she had to be strong to make it in the world. He would hear his mother talking to her about God and his love for her.

It took a while, but eventually, she came around and began to trust him. That's how they became friends. After the cycle was broken, Mother started getting up and helping Aunt Neva around the house.

Before she sought outside jobs, she gave 100 percent at the house. She began to feel like the sister he had never had.

Even though our mother often shared her story with Bernie, sometimes he listened, but most of the time, he would turn the conversation in another direction. He never stopped telling his jokes, and eventually, she began to laugh. Bernie asked our mom why she had laughed so much. She explained that she was tired of walking around with her head hanging down. She was tired of hidden and silent tears. He was glad to see this side of our mother. She decided that if she had to cry, she would also pray. She said that she would hold her head up high and more importantly, she would keep praying.

I journaled about the information Bernie had provided. I wrote down the way that I felt and my perception of the way that Mother must have felt. She was conflicted because of her fear, and she was learning how to be faithful. These words came into my mind. She needed to stay focused on where the Master was.

WHERE THE MASTER IS

Look up! Don't hang your head down.
Hold your head up high.
Look to the hills where the Master is
Even if you must cry.

It's okay if you must shed a tear.
Your humanity allows you to feel.
Pour out your heart to where the Master is
Because He can help you heal.

After the tears, comes the healing,
And your way, you can finally see.
Look to the hills where the Master is.
Thank Him for his grace and mercy.

He said, "Let not your heart be troubled."
He'll make your burdens light.
Look to the hills where the Master is.
He'll help you win this fight.

6

VIOLA REVEALS A SECRET

(Reflection 2)

Viola was Mark and Hazel's oldest child. She was bold and carefree. She was the daughter whom Mark loved and allowed to stay in the household. In the early 1900s, Viola was able to survive the turbulence and all Mark's rants. Was this because she was the firstborn, or was this because she was the favored child?

Viola was a couple of years older than Mother. They resembled each other in many ways. However, Viola was bold and raw while Mother was more reserved.

I remember a conversation that I had with Viola's daughter, Irene. We discussed our mothers. Irene's mother often talked about how she and our mom were raised separately. As a young girl, she couldn't understand the reason why, at times, their dad would not let Junior, my mother, and her play together or have any communication. He didn't treat her well but fussed at Destine a lot. She couldn't understand why. Viola often felt sorry for Mother because many times, she was alone.

Viola also felt bad about the way their dad talked to Mother and made her feel so low. He picked on her often and mocked her most of the time. Mother did her chores and kept her mouth shut according to Viola. Mark taunted our mother repeatedly. Irene said her mother resented it, but it was hard for her to stand up for our mother. Mark started talking in what sounded like a demonic language. Viola could not tell where it was coming from.

Once, Viola had seen Mark and another man laughing and joking according to Irene. It had turned into an argument quickly. Mark was arguing and stuttering to the point that her mother didn't know what he was talking about. He reached for his knife and threatened to stab the man if he didn't get out of his yard.

Viola had many lonely days without Mother. There were times after Mother had left when Viola missed her sister so much. Every chance she got, she went over to Aunt Neva's house to bond with her, but she knew Mother couldn't come back home.

Irene said that Viola and Mother shared secrets. Her mother told her about the time she had told our mother that they had another sister. When she told Mother this, Viola also asked her not to say anything about it because she would get in trouble. Once she told Mother about this, she was afraid. Our mother was always good at keeping secrets because she had been threatened so much not to tell. Viola had to hold many secrets too. Our mother wanted to know why another sister was a secret.

According to Irene, Viola was nervous because she had leaked the information to my mother. One day, Viola said she met Bernie Lee while walking. He approached her and said that Destine told him she might have another sister. He also said when he asked her to repeat herself, she shrugged away and got quiet.

Viola became very nervous because she figured if Mother was talking to Bernie about what she had heard, it was just a matter of time before things got out of hand. Viola knew how Bernie Lee loved to talk and ask questions.

Viola made another visit to Aunt Neva's house after getting the news from Bernie Lee. Viola had pleaded with our mother to leave it alone until she could get more information. She told our mother to keep her eyes and ears open.

Irene asked me if our mother had ever told us this before. I told her that I had never heard it explained this way.

Later that night after talking to Irene, I summarized our conversation in my head. I started thinking that Mark must have seen something special in Mother that he resented. I believe that he saw qualities in her that he envied and wished that he had. I believe that he wanted to break her. I also believe my mother was the black sheep of the family.

BLACK SHEEP

The black sheep is the different one
From all others in the flock.
She stands out without a doubt.
This sheep, they will mock.

They mock her when she does right,
But righteousness she tries to own.
Because they can't see as she sees,
She usually stands alone.

She's mocked when she tries to keep the peace,
And misunderstood whenever she speaks.
Truth is spoken without the coats of sugar;
Gently spoken, but she's not weak.

She's mocked, but she's reliable.
With endurance she won't stray.
She consistently fulfills her duties
Because she knows that this is the way.

She is mocked and taunted with rejection,
But she waits and waits patiently.
She prays, she trusts, and she holds on
Because one day she knows she'll be free.

7

WHAT DAD KNEW FIRST

Dad told us that he had known Mother had another sister before she ever found out. He said that Bernie Lee had informed him of the situation because he overheard Aunt Neva and Uncle Simon talking about it. According to Dad, our mother, Destine and her sister Patience were raised in different backgrounds. Dad said he was shocked when he found out this information, especially the part about them being twins. He said they were separated when they were born.

Aunt Elizabeth, who was Dad's biological aunt, took Patience and raised her as her own in Virginia. Aunt Elizabeth had married into wealth, and her husband had died and left her with a decent estate. This caused Aunt Elizabeth to think that she was better than the rest of the family, but she too tried to cover up a secret.

Mark didn't want our mother in his home, and he didn't want her twin either. Hazel felt that if she gave the child away, it would cause less confusion in the home. Mark didn't think the children were his.

Patience had a good life with Aunt Elizabeth. Because Aunt Elizabeth didn't have children of her own, she afforded Patience just about anything she wanted, including a high school education.

Bernie had often wondered why Mother had not put these things together. Aunt Elizabeth always stayed at Aunt Neva's with Patience every time they came to North Carolina. At least that should have aroused our mother's suspicion because she was very wise about a lot of things.

Destine and Patience, (Hessa and Sahana, respectively) got along very well. Bernie heard them sharing information about their lives. He noticed many similarities between the two, but he didn't want to get involved. It was so clear to him that they were related, even though they were not identical. They were beautiful brown girls with long black hair. He was nervous that the truth would come out at any given time when they visited.

The girls growing up with two different last names and in different environments may have been the hindrance that kept them in the dark. Destine grew up with the last name of Murcel, and Patience's last name was Brinson. Neither his mom nor Aunt Elizabeth openly told the girls how closely related they were. Bernie thought that they felt guilty about this, but at least, they allowed them to be together.

Bernie had seen the girls secretly listening to Neva and Elizabeth. He wanted them to eavesdrop enough so that they would find out what he knew. He even started feeling guilty around the girls because he wasn't sure whether they had heard enough to piece things together.

Mom's life was much simpler than Patience's life was. Aunt Neva, Bernie, and Uncle Simon agreed that Mother was very wise and had a great sense of direction. They also agreed that she was very spiritual and depended on God for her guidance.

Because of his visits to Aunt Neva's, Dad knew that Mother's life was very challenging. Aunt Neva told Dad and Bernie that Hazel would have kept her if she could but when things got so rough around the house, she let her go to minimize confusion in the home.

Aunt Neva explained to Dad that Mother grew up in an environment of fear, suffering, and despair. She further said that she was unable to get the education that she so desperately wanted but that she was blessed with wisdom. Aunt Neva observed her enough to know that Mother had been misunderstood, accused, and abused. Our mother had a lot of hopes and dreams. Aunt Neva knew in her heart that she would have better days.

Destine loved her mother, but at times, she loathed her father because he always made her feel inadequate and enjoyed publicly denouncing her. Her parents had some issues, as well as her younger brother June. Mom's understanding was different than theirs was. Our mother could not get over the fact that her dad loved June and her sister Viola. She did understand that their normal was not her normal. Her goal was always to be good enough and acceptable so that she would have a stable place to stay.

Even though there were many challenges, Bernie believed that she was smart enough and knew and understood what was really going on. Because he and our mother were related and were friends, he became tired of holding it all in. He had never been able to hold anything in as long as he had held this information. Bernie wasn't the type to bring up anything.

8

A MOMENT OF TRUTH

Dad told us how everything had finally unfolded. I think he told us because he felt that we really needed to understand our mother more and the things that made her who she was. Aunt Neva and Uncle Simon had really begun aging. Bernie Lee had gotten married and moved up north after he had left the military. He didn't come home that often. Because both of his parents were ill at around the same time, they needed someone to look after them.

During this time in the 1930s, Mom and Dad had gotten married. Even though they were young, they were responsible. They were in the process of starting a family.

After a lengthy illness, Uncle Simon died. Our mom felt that they should take Aunt Neva into their home. Without hesitation, they took her in. Dad's own mother, Marie, was aging as well. Aunt Neva wanted to keep her house. She also wanted Marie to come and live with her. Instead, my parents took both women in so that they could take care of them.

Many times, Dad said he felt guilty for not telling Mother what he knew about her family secret because it was not his story to tell. Our mom spent a lot of time with Aunt Neva and our grandmother. Our grandmother was very helpful around the house because she was not as sickly as Aunt Neva was. With the help of our grandmother, they kept Aunt Neva clean, fed, and loved. Dad said our mother wanted to do unto Aunt Neva as she had done for her in her early life. Mother felt guilty even though she was doing good deeds. It was hard to explain.

Mother and Aunt Neva had many conversations during their time together. Aunt Neva was always giving Mother advice. As Aunt Neva's health started deteriorating, their relationship got even closer.

One evening, Aunt Neva called my mom and dad into the room. She wanted to tell them something. She stressed that it was very important. As Mother waited for Aunt Neva to speak, she began to gasp. She was very weak, and her voice came out as a whisper.

She finally explained that she was waiting for her sister Elizabeth to come before she said anything. Then Aunt Neva decided to go ahead and tell them. Because he knew, he could only hope that things would go well.

Aunt Neva didn't hesitate. She immediately told our mom that she and Patience were sisters. She further told her that they were not only sisters but twins. Aunt Neva explained that since Hazel had given Patience away as a baby, everyone had agreed it would be too confusing to explain. It would be better to let the two of them grow up as cousins. Aunt Neva also explained that she knew my mom had been going through much. She and everyone involved hadn't wanted to burden her with something she couldn't change.

As Aunt Neva was telling our mom about her sister, tears fell from her eyes. Dad said that Mom didn't ask any questions. She didn't make any comments at all. She just listened. It had gone well. Mother didn't show any anger toward Aunt Neva. Mother felt that Aunt Neva was the closest thing to a mother that she had ever had. She was good to her. Mother had a lot of respect for Aunt Neva. Dad believed that Mom had let her speak her peace because Aunt Neva was getting weaker and was trying to get her house in order.

Aunt Neva and Aunt Elizabeth had discussed the situation and felt it was time to tell the sisters the truth. They felt they were old enough to understand what had happened and why it had happened. Aunt Neva also felt that all three sisters should have a closer relationship. Even though they were grown-ups, it was time to help fill the void in their lives.

Our mother remained silent and eventually excused herself from the room. After she had exited, Aunt Neva motioned him to come over to her bed. He didn't know what to expect because it had been so emotional. Aunt Neva made an emotional plea for him to take care of our mom and to be good to her. She reminded him that our mom had been through so much. She said that Mom had come from a world of confusion and that she needed a lot of love. Aunt Neva said that as her favorite nephew, she was depending on him to handle the situation with care. He made a promise to her that he would.

After several days had passed, Mother remained quiet, and she was very distant. As Dad watched her, she seemed to be in a daze. Even though she continued doing what she had to do around the house, she appeared to be in entranced.

Dad gave her a few days, and then he decided to talk with our mother to see exactly where her head was. What came next nearly broke him down, but he knew that he had to remain strong for our mother. She poured out her feelings to him. In tears, she expressed how she felt like she couldn't get a break. She said that she was so full of mixed emotions and confusion that she couldn't breathe.

She spoke about how complicated her life seemed. She felt like she had never had a real mother or father. She had heard rumors of another sister, but even that had been kept a secret. Even though she had many siblings, she didn't have a real connection or relationship with any of them.

She was glad that Aunt Neva had finally told her the truth. It was one less burden that she had to carry. She no longer had to wonder about it. Mother said that the days she had kept to herself, she had been crying, praying, and meditating. She had been overwhelmed, and she had needed to find some quietness and peace.

She assured my dad that she would be all right. She also told him something she had carried for a long time. When she had first moved in with Aunt Neva, she had been going through a rough period. Aunt Neva had reminded her that she had to be patient and obedient and to persevere. These words were a part of her everyday life. They were in her heart and spirit. She lived by them.

Mother knew that her dad didn't acknowledge her as his child. If that was the case, he felt the same way about Patience (Sahana). While on the subject, she still couldn't figure out why they had given Patience away as a baby and had kept her to live a life of suffering.

When Aunt Neva talked to our mother, things calmed down some. However, about three weeks later, Aunt Elizabeth and Patience came to visit Aunt Neva. When they arrived, they found that Aunt Elizabeth was feeble as well. As soon as Aunt Elizabeth walked into the house, Aunt Neva perked up. Patience seemed very quiet and reserved, as if she had a lot on her mind.

It became really tense in the house because everyone knew what was about to go down. After everyone was situated, Aunt Neva suddenly said that it was time to clear the air and make some wrongs right. Aunt Neva asked Aunt Elizabeth if she had done her part yet. Aunt Elizabeth assured her that she had.

Aunt Neva finally called Patience and our mom into her room, as well as Aunt Elizabeth. She asked Dad to be part of what she had to say. Aunt Neva didn't hold back. She asked Patience and Mother how they felt, now that they knew what they knew.

Patience burst into tears before Aunt Neva could say anything else. It was clear to Dad that Patience was crying because she didn't know what everyone else knew. Aunt Elizabeth looked at Aunt Neva and began swearing, cursing, asking her what she was talking about. Dad saw Aunt Elizabeth in a way that he'd never seen her before. It got so loud that Grandmother Marie came into the room to find out what had gotten into Aunt Elizabeth.

Patience was crying and panting as she asked Aunt Neva to explain what she had been talking about. Patience kept saying that according to her mom, Mother was her cousin. Aunt Neva rose up in her weak condition and asked Aunt Elizabeth if she had told Patience the truth. Aunt Neva said that she had already told our mom.

The room was filled with people who were crying. Aunt Neva and Aunt Elizabeth began crying as well. Grandmother Marie told her sisters that she had known that was going to happen. She also told them to get the matter straightened out. Our grandmother got rough with both of them.

Everything turned bad quickly. Dad had expected to see tears coming from Patience and Mother. He had also been certain that his two aunts had done their part so that things would run more smoothly, but it seemed that wasn't the case.

Dad finally intervened by asking our grandmother to take Aunt Elizabeth and Patience to another room so that he could try to help smooth things over. He also needed to calm our mother and Aunt Neva down.

Aunt Neva was very upset with Aunt Elizabeth at this point. Up until then, they had always been very close. He had seen the older sisters argue before, but this time, Aunt Neva seemed infuriated because Aunt Elizabeth had not fulfilled the agreement as she had promised.

Dad explained to Aunt Neva that he had watched Aunt Elizabeth as she had been talking to her, and she didn't seem herself. Aunt Elizabeth had seemed withdrawn until Patience had started crying. Dad didn't think Aunt Elizabeth had remembered to tell Patience. Aunt Neva and our mother finally stopped crying. He hugged Aunt Neva, and she seemed to calm down.

Afterward, he went into the room where Patience and Aunt Elizabeth were. Things were more dramatic in that room. Patience was crying uncontrollably, while at the same time, she was trying to calm Aunt Elizabeth down as she raged, ranted, cursed, and threatened. Dad had a tough time as he tried to talk with Aunt Elizabeth because she kept cursing and babbling, almost as if she were speaking in an unknown tongue. Every time he tried to reason with her, she got worse. Grandmother Marie finally raised her voice and told Aunt Elizabeth to hush and to get it together. His mother told her she was acting foolish.

Because he couldn't get anywhere with Aunt Elizabeth, Dad asked Patience what was going on with her mother. Patience cried out that her mother had stopped taking her medicine and that things were getting worse. Dad asked what kind of medicine she had been taking. Patience told him that her mother had been diagnosed with a terminal illness.

When Aunt Elizabeth heard those words, she started toward Patience and reached out to strike her. Dad's mother grabbed her arms and hands. They both talked to her until she came to her senses and calmed down. Even though Aunt Neva was weak, she and our mom entered the room to see what was going on. The room wasn't that large, so he motioned for them to go back out because he felt like he was getting everything under control.

Dad sat Aunt Elizabeth in a chair and asked her several questions to see how her mind was. She slowly responded to his questions and wanted to know the reason that he was talking to her in that manner.

After talking with her, he knew that she was in trouble because she was staring and acting very confused. He then called our mother into the room to make a bed up for Aunt Elizabeth so that she could lie down. Mother and Grandmother Marie helped in assisting Aunt Elizabeth into bed. Then Mother left the room. Our grandmother, Patience, and he stayed with Aunt Elizabeth until she drifted off to sleep.

Aunt Neva later began yelling for him, so he went to check on her. She wanted him to get Patience to come back in her room so that she could try to find out what was really going on with Aunt Elizabeth and to further straighten out the mess that had been created.

Patience entered the room, and Aunt Neva told her to come and sit beside her on one side and had our mother sit on the other side of her. She held both of their hands. The room was still filled with the sounds of crying. Aunt Neva told the girls that she knew they were hurting but that this had to be done. She told them that she didn't want to leave the world without telling them the truth.

It was so emotional. Aunt Neva was very compassionate. She talked to them and prayed with them. She told them that they would both be fine and explained the reason that she had waited until they were grown to tell them the story. They had been too young to know the truth, and the truth would have only complicated their lives. She believed that this was the right moment for them to know, and that in time, they would heal from this new information.

Mother seemed to handle everything well because she had had time to process what she had learned. Patience wanted further explanations even though she kept crying. Aunt Neva told Patience that her real parents were Mark and Hazel Murcel. She had been given to Elizabeth as a baby. She and our mother were twins. She had taken our mother in when she had been twelve.

Aunt Neva told Patience that Mark had been unhappy with them because he hadn't thought that they were his children. Hazel hadn't thought that it was safe to keep either of them. There had been rumors that Mark had planned to kill them if they had remained in the house. As Aunt Neva told Mom and Patience this, they both began to cry again but continued to listen.

Patience asked Aunt Neva who Hazel and Mark were. Aunt Neva told Patience that she knew who they were. They were relatives. Aunt Neva told her she hadn't been around them long enough to get to know them well.

Aunt Neva explained that Hazel was Uncle Simon's biological niece. Hazel was a good woman. She was clean and neat, but she was slow in understanding things. Her sister had experienced life with their parents. She had witnessed the threats that Mark had imposed on her daily, about her not being his child. He had felt the same way about both of them.

Aunt Neva told Patience that Mark had accused Hazel of messing around. That was why he felt the way he did. He had told Hazel that he had only had one child at the time, and she was their sister Viola.

Aunt Neva also explained that Mark was an evil man. He was selfish, mean, and full of anger. Hazel had reached out to her and explained how dangerous it was to keep the sisters there. That's when she had reached out to Elizabeth and asked her to take Patience because she hadn't had children of her own.

Patience wanted to know why she chose her and not her sister. Aunt Neva told her that Elizabeth only wanted one of them but that another relative had planned to take Mom. But as soon as they had gone to pick her up, Mark had snapped and told them they couldn't have his child. Aunt Neva wanted Patience to know that she had another sister and a younger brother. He seemed to love those two. Mark, Hazel, and Patience's brother had some issues.

After gathering this information together, I decided that secrets and hidden things might temporarily solve a problem, but in the long run, they would only cause long-term confusion. When I thought about the secrets, I contemplated the way a veil covers and hides. Then I began to write.

Wanda G. Atkinson

THE VEIL

There is more than one person in the chapel
That is covered with a veil.
They wear theirs to be obvious,
While obviously others time will tell.

The bride stands covered with anticipation.
The groom is covered with pride.
The best man stands covered there with him,
As though innocence has nothing to hide.

The honored maid is covered with dedication
To the traditions for this array.
No matter what she knows, she won't let it show
Because she's hoping this is her lucky day.

Some of the guests are well covered too,
Hiding behind whispers, gestures, and smiles.
They're pretending to be so happy for you,
While their motives show a different style.

The preacher gathers the couple together.
His cover is second to none.
Without knowing their characters or histories,
His finale is, "Now they are one."

The veil is an obvious cover.
While one is seen, others are seen through.
So if you have a place in the chapel,
Which veil is covering you?

9

MOVING FORWARD

———•◦•———

Dad told us that after everything had been exposed about our mother and Patience, they focused on getting Aunt Elizabeth straight. Aunt Elizabeth and Patience stayed with them another week before going back to Virginia. As they left, Aunt Elizabeth seemed to be fine, and Patience promised that she would stay in touch and let them know how she was progressing.

Dad wasn't sure how Patience felt because she was motionless except for promising us that she would keep in touch. He knew that she and our mother had had a close relationship before Aunt Neva had told her the whole story.

Aunt Neva started getting her strength back and miraculously got back on her feet. She felt like she was ready to be on her own again. For a while, Dad's house had become very crowded. Even though Aunt Neva was welcome in his home, he didn't argue with her about getting her own space back. About a month later, Aunt Neva got a house near him. She and our grandmother moved in together.

Dad felt that he and Mother needed some time to themselves. For about a month, Mother seemed to be less burdened. He believed that knowing the truth had really helped her. Just when things were getting on track, they got the news that Aunt Elizabeth had passed away.

Patience came home for Aunt Elizabeth's funeral. She kept her distance from the family, and she was very quiet and reserved. Our mother was able to hold it together, even after all she had learned, but Patience couldn't seem to adapt.

Bernie was very disappointed in how Patience had acted toward the family during and after the funeral. Bernie told Dad about the good times our mother and Patience used to have as girls.

Aunt Neva reminded them that Patience had been brought up in a different environment. Patience had snooty and uppity ways. She believed that Patience would eventually come around.

After this settled down and months and years had passed, it appeared that Patience had truly disconnected from the family. Acquaintances from Virginia informed them that Patience had met and married a man who was a big gambler. Aunt Elizabeth had left her estate to Patience. The acquaintances told them that her husband had gambled so much that Patience had lost her estate.

Some of the family members had not been satisfied with the information that they had received, so they went to her last known address, but it was to no avail. Patience seemed to have vanished. There were many rumors: Her new husband may have killed her and disposed of her body, or she left him because of his gambling and violent ways.

As time passed, Mother's feelings for Patience started to bother her. She told Dad that she never thought they would be any closer because of the information they had learned but that she wanted Patience to be safe. Once again, she blamed her parents for the mess and confusion.

Many of the family members believed that Patience was somewhere doing fine but not wanting any part of the new life or the new truth that she had learned. Mother was hurt, but as always, she decided to be obedient and patient and to persevere.

10

MA-REE'S REFLECTION

(Reflection 3)

Our Grandmother Marie, whom we called Ma-Ree, filled in a lot of blanks for us. She was around us a lot because she truly loved us. After everything had settled down from the secrets being revealed, Dad and Mother were finally able to start their family. Ma-Ree told us that once the children had come, our mother had seemed more at ease. She believed that Mother had been happy to be able to call something her own.

Mother was devoted to us and wanted only the best for each child. Even though Daddy and Mother didn't have very much, they were good at providing for the family. At times, Ma-Ree would watch our mother, especially as we children got into all kinds of things. Mother handled us with grace, but she was fussy in the good and bad times.

Our mother would often tell her that she wanted her children to do better and to have better than she had in life. Mother was very particular when it came to her children. She didn't want just anyone looking after her children, but she trusted Ma-Ree because she demonstrated her passion and love for us.

Ma-Ree came to live with Dad and Mother after Bernie Lee came to get Aunt Neva so that she could live with him and his family in South Carolina. Even though Mother was doing a good job, Ma-Ree was glad to help as much as she could.

Our parents had children quickly. When Ma-Ree moved back, she already had five grandchildren: three boys and two girls. Ma-Ree described us as steps because we were born one after another. After the fifth child was born, it started getting crowded.

Grandmother Hazel was failing in health, and our mother decided to take her in because her sister Viola's husband would not allow her to live with them. Grandmother Hazel tried to develop a relationship, but it was awkward because she hadn't been around that much. The children respected her, but they didn't understand her because of her speech impediment. Ma-Ree spent a lot of time with us because Mother had to pay close attention to her own mother.

Ma-Ree helped with the cooking, washing, and cleaning. She also trained the children to help. She knew how important it was for my mom to get bonding time with her own mother.

11

MORE REFLECTIONS FROM MA-REE

(Reflection 4)

Ma-Ree told us different things at different times. She told us that Aunt Neva got homesick while staying with Bernie Lee. She received a letter from Aunt Neva on a cold winter's day stating that she would be home early that spring. It did Aunt Neva's heart good to get this news. Even though she was enjoying her grandkids and doing what she could to help Mother with our other grandmother, she really missed Aunt Neva.

Later, Ma-Ree told us that while they were assisting Hazel, Viola brought news that the nursing home had contacted her and said that Mark was ailing. They informed her that he only had a few days to live. He had requested to see his children. Ma-Ree convinced Mother that she should go see him and that it might help her with some of her feelings.

Mother and Viola made the visit. Mark died the following day. At this point, they were not sure where their brother was. They gave Mark a private funeral because of the way he had treated people that they knew. They didn't tell Hazel of his passing, even though they had not lived together for many years.

As soon as spring came, Aunt Neva would be returning for sure. She wasn't the only one who was coming. When Bernie Lee drove up, they noticed that the car looked crowded. As the doors opened, Bernie Lee, his wife, Amira, and Aunt Neva got out. They saw another female figure in the car. Bernie Lee was grinning and smiling because he was excited and wanted to say who it was. After he could no longer hold it in, he blurted out that he had found Patience and that she was with him.

Everyone seemed to be glad to see each other. Ma-Ree told Patience to come on in, but she was very cautious and came in slowly. As Mother came in from the back of the house, everyone in the room became very silent. Bernie Lee jumped up and hugged Mother tightly. Mother hugged Aunt Neva and Amira. Mother looked at Patience as Bernie Lee told her to look at whom he had found. The sisters spoke, but they were very cautious around one another. Their relationship was nothing like it had been when they were younger.

Aunt Neva and the others didn't know that Hazel was at the house until Ma-Ree told them. Patience looked as if she had seen a ghost after hearing this information. Aunt Neva asked our mother to go with her to see Hazel. They asked Patience to join them, but she remained seated.

As she stayed with the others, Bernie Lee told Dad that he needed to talk with him privately. When they returned, they brought in the luggage. Bernie Lee and Amira proceeded to where Hazel was. After a very short visit, they began saying their goodbyes.

Dad asked Mother to step outside with him after Bernie Lee had left. He explained that Aunt Neva and Patience would be staying with them until he could find them a house. Mother was not happy with the idea, especially since Aunt Neva had told her that Patience had suffered a nervous breakdown and had had some other illnesses. Mother was concerned about the children and everyone else in the house.

Aunt Neva explained how they had found Patience. Bernie Lee had an acquaintance at his work, who kept talking about a lady that he was dating named Patience. When Bernie Lee heard that name, he began asking questions until he knew that it was she. The acquaintance told him that he wanted her out of his house. The man said that he was not the type of person to take care of a sick woman.

Aunt Neva and Patience stayed with my parents for about two months. This gave Patience a chance to get to know Hazel a little bit better. This also gave Mother a chance to spend more time with her children. Patience was distant and quiet, but during her stay, she helped with Hazel. Between Mother, Viola, and Patience, they were able to give Hazel good care, and they even bonded a little.

After Dad found a house for Aunt Neva and Patience, they continued to come by daily to help with Hazel. Patience seemed happier after they moved out. She seemed to be adjusting to her new life.

About a month after the two had settled into their home, Hazel took a turn for the worse and died. Mother and Viola were incredibly sad. Immediately after the funeral, Patience became ill with flu-like symptoms. Patience was restless and feverish throughout the night.

The next day after taking her to the doctor, she was given a shot for the flu. The shot was apparently too strong for her. She lost her voice, she could no longer swallow, and she began foaming at the mouth. Ma-Ree, Mother, and Viola were all there to help Aunt Neva. They

59

watched Patience get weaker and sicker. Before they could get her back to the doctor, she too died a week after Hazel had died. Mother and Viola cried hysterically. With so much grief so close together, it dismayed them.

After they had the funeral for Patience, Aunt Neva moved back in with them until she could assess her living arrangements. However, the grief did not end there. The authorities contacted Mother and Viola to inform them that their brother Mark Jr. (June Boy) had been found dead in a rundown house in a neighboring city. This happened one month later. Yet again, they were both distraught because they had not heard from him and had not known how to reach him.

12

DELIVERANCE

According to the earlier stories that we were told about our mother and the little bit she shared, she had really come a long way. However, as Mother's life started getting better, she began to tell us more about her upbringing. We attributed her opening up to us as her gaining confidence and holding onto her faith. We, her children, knew that even though she had shared new information, there was still much left to our imaginations.

She told us how lost and lonely she had felt as a young girl. No matter which way she turned, she sometimes felt blocked and closed in. She kept believing there was a way out, but at the same time, she wasn't completely sure how. Because there was so much uncertainty, she was fearful most of the time. Something on the inside kept pushing her not to give up, so she kept pressing on and praying in the best way she knew how.

She had felt caught between two worlds. On the one hand, she had been surrounded with havoc and confusion, which had nearly broken her. Yet she had known that she couldn't afford to allow her circumstances to break her completely. She had needed to keep pressing on. On the other hand, she had needed to keep looking forward to a better day, despite her feelings and emotions.

Even though she grew up to be a loner, she somehow knew that she was not alone. She believed that her life was meant to be as it had been so that she could get a sense of whom God was. Even though she hadn't been afforded a proper education, through her loneliness, she had gained wisdom and strength in her weakest moments. She had always tried to be obedient and good, but no matter what she had done, it had never been good enough in that environment.

Aunt Neva had been her ray of light, which God had given her when Aunt Neva had taken her in. With her, she had found a sense of peace.

Mom often told us how unstable her life had been before she moved in with Aunt Neva. She had had no idea how things were going to work out because of the traumatic life she had experienced. She said that her state of mind had been like that of an animal caught in a snare.

With Aunt Neva, she had begun to get some focus. It wasn't noisy there. She was able to think more clearly, she could finally breathe, and she didn't have to constantly look over her shoulder.

Even though it was a new life, Mother didn't miss the environment she had lived in. She did miss her family, especially her mother. Although she had lived in fear during her first twelve years of life, she still loved and missed her mother and siblings.

She had mixed emotions while living at Aunt Neva's house. The quietness was something she had to adjust to. At night, she thought on many things. She also spent time talking with the Lord. Many times, Aunt Neva would ask her who she was talking to when she openly spoke and poured her heart out to the Lord.

Before she had left home, she had silently asked the Lord to help her. That had been the sum of her prayers. At Aunt Neva's, she was able to kneel, pray, and talk comfortably with God. She fell on her face before Him daily, seeking His voice. She knew she had a purpose. She wanted to know they way that she should go.

It seemed that every time Mother would share with us, it allowed me to be empathetic towards her. My imagination would lead me to my tablet, and I would get into writing mode. I wrote what I felt that Mom was saying when she spoke from her heart. I think in the following poem, she was talking about her deliverance.

DELIVERANCE

I am lost but want to be found
Out of the maze that I am in.
I go north, south, east, and west,
Yet all I can find is sin.

I keep seeking the direction
To a path that's clean and clear.
Right when I think that I have found it,
There's more sin, which causes more fear.

I spring forth, and then I fall back.
Deeper into the maze, I go.
Feeling trapped and without an exit,
My self-esteem is mighty, mighty low.

I persevere, going forth and falling back.
I press with all my might,
Feeling weak but strong enough to know
That I want to see the light.

I finally get a ray of light
From a trip that's been dark and hollow.
I now see a friend, an everlasting friend,
A friend that will lead and that I can follow.

13

REFLECTIONS OF ANGELS

Ma-Ree had been a part of our family for as long as I can remember. Even though I was young, I can still remember what a great grandmother she was. I remember everything she taught us. I was curious, and I retained more information than I care to remember.

When Ma-Ree became ill, Mother and my sister Hana took care of her. Mother and Ma-Ree had a great relationship. Even though Ma-Ree was strong and a fighter, she was stricken with a terminal illness. In those days, children didn't know about those types of things because we weren't supposed to listen. However, I listened and understood things at a very early age.

Ma-Ree was bedridden for about two years. She died in her sleep. She was only in her early sixties. It was a great loss around our house because she had been part of our family. She had really helped Mother take care of us for many years. Even though she was Dad's mother, he and Mother were both devastated. Dad, Mother, and Aunt Neva never spoke much about Ma-Ree. They apparently kept their feelings to themselves. I can imagine how numb Mother must have felt.

During the early seventies, Mom was had to face the fact that her sister Viola had been diagnosed with a terminal illness. Viola's sickness was progressive, and it took her quickly. In less than a year, she died suddenly.

During the next couple of years, the family found out that Aunt Neva had been secretly seeing a doctor. She had withheld information from the family that the doctor had advised her on. She had begun to have fainting spells on a regular basis. Even though she had been living on her own, she had begun spending more time with us.

Aunt Neva had loved Dad and Mother, and they had looked up to her. She had been a fighter like Ma-Ree had been. She had held strong until her heart had given out. She had died as a fighter.

Once again, my parents were lost. Mother felt that everyone who had helped her keep it together before was now leaving her.

14

THE HOMEMAKER

Even though Mother went through a lot on a daily basis, she was a wonderful homemaker. Mom seemed most content with her life when she was doing things that she could do well. There were at least three things that she took pride in. They were cooking, washing, and quilting. These things meant a lot to her, and she had enough practice in life to do them well.

When it came to cooking, she could compete with the best of them. Our family was large, and some of us didn't eat the same things. Mother would prepare a regular meal and something for the finicky eaters as well. Many times, we had widowed men, neighborhood children raised without women in the home, or random visitors sharing a meal with us. She would always tell us that food was meant to be shared and that it was not right to deny people, especially when they were hungry.

Just in case one of us didn't see it her way, she would tell us to never hurt anyone's feelings where food was concerned. We didn't know when we might get into a situation where we were hungry and someone might have to reach out to us.

I remember neighbors asking her to cook specific meals, such as a pan of biscuits, a pot of pork neck bones, or even a pan of fried chicken. She was more than happy to oblige. It seems that it gave her a sense of peace to help the less fortunate because she understood their feelings and ways of life.

She took pride in cooking. She was a great cook and soaked in every compliment that she was given. Without being arrogant, Mother gave a tiny smile when she was given a compliment that was related to her cooking. Every now and then, I would offer to assist her in cooking and preparing meals. She would allow me to watch over the food that was cooking, but she did the honors of starting and completing the meals.

Mother knew how we, as her children, loved and enjoyed her cooking, but anyone was welcome to her food. A visitor could make mention of a specific dish that he or she wished for, and she would send my dad or one of us to the store to purchase the ingredients so that she could cook the suggested item. Mother cooked many collard greens for us, as well as other people. She made potato puddings and pies at the request of many people and for many occasions. It always made Mother feel good to share her food. It was as if it blessed her to share.

She also loved washing things. Many times, my sister and I would offer to give her a break and do the washing ourselves. Mother wouldn't hear of it. We felt guilty having Mother do our clothes, but she wanted to do it and acted as if she didn't mind at all. My sister and I often said to each other that Mother didn't think that we could wash as well as she did. She had her own way of separating, folding, and ironing the clothes.

As far back as I can remember, Mother had been making quilts. It seemed to be an art for her. Since we had such a large family, she made sure there were enough quilts for everyone during the winter months.

Quilting was an art that she learned from Aunt Neva at an early age. I remember visiting Aunt Neva's and watching her and Mother create patterns of the quilts they would make. Mother created an overflow of quilts. Her quilts were of good quality. She put a lot of time and effort into making the quilts. The overflow allowed her to give quilts to her children and grandchildren. Many vowed that they would hold on to them for the rest of their lives.

Mother had always been the manager of our household. She trained us girls in how to keep a house. If it wasn't up to par, she would go behind us to fix things to her satisfaction.

She loved keeping busy. She was constantly sweeping, closing drawers (she hated clothes hanging out of drawers), and mopping. Mother would quickly let us know that even if we thought we were grown, we would never take over her position.

We didn't want Mother to run herself down, but she always wanted to keep busy. Every once and a while, we would tease her and call her a busy bee. However, she didn't like that because Mother wanted us to always understand that her position was as our mother, which she took very seriously.

15

YOU ARE WELCOME

When our family was together, Mother often talked about how happy she had felt when each of us had entered the world. She told us that when it came to her kids, we mattered much to her. All of us were very protective of Mother because of her past. Our dad was as well.

Although she and Dad instilled in us the best that they could offer, every now and then, some of us messed up. We exhibited forms of rebellion but felt guilt and shame afterward.

Mother prided herself on being the matriarch of our family. In retrospect, she appropriately enjoyed tasks that included being a wife, mother, homemaker, advisor, counselor, teacher, and so much more. In all this, she clearly was the manager of our home. She was adamant that we grow up at a certain pace. She wanted us to remember our places and that we would never be grown enough to take over.

Mother excelled in two special areas that she held near and dear to her heart. Those specialties were cooking and quilting. Mother ruled the kitchen. There were times when we had more than enough to eat and other times when there was not as much. Her skills would allow her to make a little become much.

As I said earlier, because Mother prided herself on cooking, anyone (not only her children) at any time could request a certain type of food (a specialty for example), and she would immediately gather the necessary ingredients to fulfill the request. She loved sharing her food. She believed that she welcomed others when she shared what she had been gifted to do.

She always kept busy. During her downtime, she loved to make quilts. Throughout her lifetime, she made them well. The artistry and designs of her quilts showed her love and sentiment to the receiver.

Family was precious to Mother. She didn't take anything about us for granted. Rather, she embraced the good and bad and maintained that she was well pleased and destined to fulfill the duties of a wife and mother. She also maintained that no matter how hard or overwhelmed she got at times, it was her duty to do her responsibilities as a child of God. Through it all, she welcomed her family, visitors, and life.

16

REFLECTIONS OF A VIRTUOUS WOMAN

Dad and Mother were hush-hush when we inquired about their relationship and their humble beginnings. We could listen to them agree to disagree all day long, but they were very evasive when it came to the affairs of the heart. However, it didn't take a genius to see that they were the loves of each other's lives. Daddy honored Mother, and Mother honored Daddy.

Mother's tone usually sounded as if she was arguing. She would make a statement, and if she didn't get a favorable response, she'd rant and rave about it (so it seemed). Dad would quietly wait it out. His patience with her was impeccable. I think Dad spoiled Mom early on because of the state she was in when he met her. He also knew that she was a good woman and a good wife.

As her children, we knew her rants were harmless. We became used to them. We knew she was a good mother.

Mother never called Dad by his real name, which was Thaddeus. However, she could really sing his nickname, which was Tad. She loved and honored him unconditionally. When Dad was away from home for any reason, Mother made sure that his food was set aside and that the house was in order when he returned. She had respect for him in and out of season.

Mother often reminded us not to bother our father when he first entered the house because she respected the fact that he was probably tired. Mother prepared our dad's favorite meals, but she didn't stop there. She would also prepare meals that we all enjoyed.

Mother came from an era where children were taught morals and were taught to live by the Golden Rule. In most cases, disrespect was not part of our upbringing. Once she had laid out the rules for our family, it only required tweaking later on. We were taught to respect our parents and any other adult. We grew up going to church. We were taught to love one another and to stay out of trouble.

Although our family was very large, Mother learned how to compartmentalize each of our issues and to deal with them accordingly. For the most part, we remained unified as a family.

Outwardly, Mother was a beautiful brown-skinned woman. Her skin was very smooth, and as she aged, she seemed to remain wrinkle free. Aside from her outward appearance, she had inner beauty. We knew she could only do so much, but she was very compassionate toward us all. She always did her best to oblige us in the most tactful manner possible.

Early on, we heard about our mother's ethics regarding hard work. Our family knew this well. We watched her and saw how she persevered by doing good. Whatever Mother did for us or others, she did it tirelessly and graciously. Her goal was to give her best.

For as long as I can remember, Mother had a close walk with the Lord. This part of her life gave her meaning and self-worth. Being a Christian added value to her life and allowed her to live unselfishly. Mother believed in sowing seeds of kindness in any setting. She often reminded us that if we would remain patient, as she had been taught at an early age, we would begin to experience and reap the promises of God.

We often saw Mother raising her hands and praising God for what He had done in her life. She was thankful for all of us and felt blessed that we made a difference in her life. A number one mother deserved the best that we had to offer. Each of us in our own way made sure that we provided Mother with our best.

17

COUNTING BLESSINGS ONE BY ONE

Through all the troubles and woes that Mother carried with her daily, she was determined to see that all her children would have a better life than she had experienced. She would often admit that raising us wasn't an easy task because as the family grew, she noticed that each of us was different. She learned good and bad things about us daily. Our different types of personalities kept her on her toes. She never expected to have such a large family because she and Daddy had come from small families.

Every now and then, Mother surprised us with things that had happened in her early life. For example, she told us that she had had five miscarriages before a child had survived. She attributed them to the beatings that she had suffered from her father.

She also told us that Dad had brought a young girl into their home named Nita Johns, whom they had raised as their own. She had been a distant relative of our dad's. Dad explained that their situations hadn't been that different because she too had not been welcomed in her mother's home. He explained that the young girl had been abused mentally and physically.

Once Mom and Dad's first child survived, the rest of her pregnancies were equally successful. She constantly told people that she had children during the early forties up until the early sixties. She told us that she felt so blessed to have us.

Even though there was ten of us (six boys and four girls), Mother was able to be a wife, mother, and homemaker and to work side by side with our father on the farm, which they had purchased together.

She often told us and we witnessed for ourselves that every day was a test. She had kept her sanity because of the gift of God's grace. God had seen her through the good and bad times.

In our household, Mother nurtured and clung to one big pet peeve. We heard it often. Each of us had to get at least a high school education. Her lack of education made it a big deal for us to succeed. Mother told us that if she was blessed to get one of us through school, she knew that she would be able to do the same for the rest of us.

The manifestation of this began when our oldest brother Tucker (Tuck) graduated. I think Mother was crossing her fingers and praying that we would follow his lead. He enrolled in college but decided that it was not for him. He loved adventure, so he later enlisted in the military. He married and started a family soon after that.

While he was still serving in the military, Tuck unexpectedly died. Mother and the family were devastated. Mother was extremely strict with and very particular about her children; therefore, it broke her heart when Tuck had left the fold. She kept busy as usual, but the family knew this really affected her deeply, as well as the rest of the family.

Hana-Joi, our oldest sister, graduated a couple of years after Tucker. She was very proper, giving, and creative, especially in the kitchen. She was our mother's right hand in that regard. Hana stayed home for a while and found a job working as a secretary at a car dealership.

While at the dealership, she met the love of her life. Mother was none too happy, but Hana had fallen in love. Ironically, Hana's love interest was quite savvy where business was concerned, which was a plus.

After they had dated and married, they moved out of state and started three businesses, which included a car dealership, a used-tire business, and a small restaurant. They started their family soon after that.

Again, Mother was heartbroken because it was hard for her to let go. We had been so tightly knitted together that it was hard on all of us, especially Dad because Hana was his favorite. One of us graduated every two or three years. Our parents had had us either two or three years apart.

Theo was the next to graduate. He immediately enlisted in the military. He wanted a new life. He wanted to see the world and learn new things. Mother was especially heartbroken about Theo because he was always quiet and shy, and he didn't know a lot of people.

Our dad had to reassure her that he would be fine. He understood that he wanted to be a man, and the military was a good place to help him in that area. After Theo had served his term, he returned home and pursued a career in law enforcement. He eventually married and started his family.

Titus (Ty) graduated two years later. Ty remained at home one more year. He was a fast talker, overly protective, and a lover of nature. He was restless because he was without his two older brothers. Ty soon met the love of his life. He and she fell head over heels in love. They started their family soon after they married.

Ty and his new wife lived in a nearby community. They both found great jobs. Ty pursued his dream of becoming a trucker while his wife worked for the local post office. Mother thought he was too young for marriage, but he still lived nearby where she could see him as often as she wanted to.

Halise (Hali) graduated two years later with honors. Hali was very smart. She was attached to both of our parents. Even though she wanted to further her education, she didn't want our parents to have to struggle so that she could go to college. She too got a job with the local post office. While she worked, she was able to pursue her dream of becoming a nurse. She started her family much later.

Taden (Tad) graduated two years after Hali. He always had an entrepreneurial mindset. Tad remained at home until he found employment with a very prestigious company that paid extremely well. However, he eventually started an auto-body shop, which was very beneficial for him. He got married, and he began his family.

I, Harmony, graduated a couple of years after Tad. I began my education at a local community college. Since I was tired of school, I found employment at the same local post office for a while. As I tried to find my way, I was blessed to work at many interesting jobs.

In the back of my mind, I still wanted to complete my education. I kept starting and stopping. As time moved on, I finally graduated from a university (the first in the family) with a degree in business management and education.

After teaching high school for a while, I began teaching at a community college. I had always had the desire to write, so I decided to pursue writing on the side.

Our youngest sister, Havana, was supposed to have been next in line to graduate, but she was stricken with an incurable illness that ended her life in the early sixties, which left Mother and the rest of the family devastated again.

Talbot (Tab) graduated three years after I did. He stayed at home until he found suitable employment with a prestigious company that paid well. He eventually established a successful welding business. Even though Tab loved our mom dearly, he moved out of the house and on his own; however, he came by every day. He later found the love of his life, settled down, and began his family.

Trenton (Trent), our youngest brother and the baby of the family, was the last to graduate, three years after Tab did. Trent always wanted to be an achiever. He liked the things that I did in life. He entered college after graduation. He stopped for a while. When he got serious, he graduated from the same university that I had. Trent got married, and he started his family much later. He became a physical education teacher and a coach, which he was very passionate about.

Mother felt that she and Daddy had really accomplished something as they watched each of us (from the late fifties to the late seventies) meet the goal that they had set before us. Mother would often tell us that we might not be able to keep up with the Joneses, but we would always get the necessities.

Through it all, Mother loved her children. That love transcended down to her grandchildren, great grandchildren, and great, great grandchildren. She would raise four of her grandsons. She took honor in doing so because it all related back to being patient and obedient and persevering.

18

THE CIRCLE OF MISSING LINKS

Mother was destined to have many friends. She was friendly, and she always did what she could to help others. Aside from our dad, she was friendly with Dad's relatives. She loved them, and they loved her.

The circle of friends that she was closest to did everything together. They all had many things in common. They all had several children, they all shared the same kind of work ethics, and they all went to the same community church. They participated in special events together. This allowed them to have bonding time, fellowship, and complete their mission at the same time. This caring group brought something to the table and most of the time, took something away. Many times, it wasn't physical but personal.

Amazingly, Mother's friends knew her story and the way that it had affected her but accepted her as she was. Although they had their own stories, their outcomes were a little different from hers.

Mother loved her biological family, but she had a strong connection with two of Dad's female cousins, as well as Dad himself. The four of them were a team.

Birdie was one of Mother's best friends. They had so much in common. They both had several children, they were sisters in Christ, and they talked and visited each other on a regular basis. Birdie was a beautiful dark-skinned woman, whose spirit kept Mother upbeat because she was very humorous and fun to be around. Most of all, she supported Mother and didn't judge her.

Gracie was another friend who brought joy into Mother's life. She was beautiful naturally and spiritually. She was sweet and understanding. They shared a special bond, and they too were sisters in Christ.

Mother also shared a close relationship with her biological cousin Roman and his wife, Myra. They too supported each other. Aside from their Christian lives, they were usually in accord on many things, especially regarding how they raised their large families. They understood each other and spoke the same language on many issues.

As time would have it, they started aging and ailing. They all cared about what happened to one another. They were there for each other. They all had lived long enough to know that death would surely come at some point.

Mother was devastated when Gracie died after a brief illness in the early 1980s. About two years later, Birdie died from a terminal illness. Even though Mother watched them both deteriorate, she stuck closely to them, even to the end. By that time, she was feeling some of her old self coming back, but she knew that even in this, she had to be patient, to obey, and to persevere.

She was almost numb by the time her cousin Roman died, which was shortly after Birdie. His wife, Myra, followed soon after that. After the passing of their friends so close together, she and Dad became even closer. They leaned on each other even more.

Years passed, and things calmed down, only to flare up again in the early 1990s. Dad had been diagnosed with a terminal illness that had been in remission for at least ten years. When it reoccurred, it began taking its toll. As he remained faithful, he got weaker. We watched Mother as she watched him. As he bore his pains, Mother's spirit began to break.

As she tried to live up to the concept of being patient and obedient and persevering, she found herself weakening. No matter how she really felt, she would always approach Dad as if she was strong and okay.

Dad started preparing my sister Hali and me without our mother's knowledge. He reminded us to take care of her and to do right by her. He reminded us of her rocky past. He also explained how far she had come since she had been mistreated by her father.

Mother kept trying to encourage Dad not to give up. Although he didn't want to give up, he had no more strength to go on. Mother stayed hopeful, but we could tell that she knew his time was nearing. In his moments of quietness, we gave him his space so that he might prepare with the Lord. Then he slipped away.

TO SEEK HIS FACE

Steal away, steal away
To a secret place.
While alone, all alone,
Trying to seek God's face.

A little room, a little room
In this congested place.
A little time, just a little time
To seek the Master's face.

A few words, just to be heard
While speaking them in haste.
I'm running a race, running a race
And seeking space to find His face.

A voice to hear, a voice to hear
Because there is no time to waste.
I'm waiting to hear, waiting to hear
That there is a place to seek His face.

19

A NEW DIMENSION TO FREEDOM

Mother was never the same again. When she finally cried out, she made it known that she had lost her best friend. Even though Mother kept trying to push through, our family knew she was losing the fight. She continued doing the things that she had always done in the house, but she was also losing her touch while doing them.

I did get a positive response from Mother when I tried to get her to write something for me. I wrote her name as a model, and she followed my example and did well. I wrote her street's name, and she did well. I finally wrote the words, "I love you," and she wrote this as well. I was amazed that she wrote these things because she hadn't practiced writing them and hadn't shown much interest in anything else. I decided to keep it as a memento.

Her health had started deteriorating after Dad's death, but she lingered on for another nine years. When she lost her mobility, life was not the same for her. Each day, Mother tried to make a comeback, but she didn't seem to be able to do it. The pace of her pushing was getting slower and slower.

At this point, the family was trying to think of ways to lift her spirits. We planned a birthday gathering for her. We invited her church family, family members that she hadn't seen in a while, and of course, our family. We made it a special day because we were celebrating her ninety-fifth birthday in August of 2009. She enjoyed the festivities, but it was clear that she was still in a state of mind that was beyond our help.

For the next four months after her birthday party, Mother's dialogue completely shifted. We noticed that she was not talking about her past. She seemed to be more focused on reminding us that she had lived a long life and that we knew she couldn't live forever.

Mother had many conversations with Hali and me, as we cared for her in her room. She talked about her love for her children and grandchildren. She said that she missed our dad and some of our other loved ones. Most of all, she talked about how thankful she was to God for the way that he had blessed her life.

When Mother and I were alone, I realized how much we connected spiritually. It was as though we had an understanding even through our eye contact. She didn't always talk. I found her watching me a lot. Sometimes she said that I reminded her of her younger self.

Mother was now trying to cling to life for her children, whom she adored. At the same time, she was trying to make peace so that she could go to the new dimension that awaited her. I felt like she was slipping away, so as sad as I was, these words came to my mind.

A NEW DIMENSION

A new dimension awaits me, a new destiny to proclaim.
It's a time to make preparations and to establish my own fame
And a time to cast away those old cares and take on cares anew.
There are no more pities and no more time to waste; that's what I used to do.
I'll wait and hope for a new hope, a hope of a new tomorrow.
With newer thoughts and newer ways, no more heartfelt sorrows.
While leaning on my helper, I'll stand tall and stand strong.
I'll cherish every minute and hope that they'll stretch long.
I'll weigh every measure and praise every breath of necessity
To reach heights and potential that were designed just for me.
Patiently, I will await, and I'll cast all my cares away.
I will aim for peace and keep praying to see that *brighter day*!

Many times, I caught her just staring. I thought that she was losing focus with the present world. I believed that a voice was whispering in her spirit and demanding her attention. As she saw us in the natural realm, she became perplexed, confused, and resistant. It appeared to be clamor: a call with two voices, perhaps, which were intertwining with her spiritual and natural state and were demanding her attention. As I watched her, everything in my spirit was telling me that she was caught in a war between two voices.

As Mother's illness progressed, she lingered in the hospital for a couple of weeks. Before she completely stopped talking, I realized (through eye contact) which voice had finally prevailed.

One by one, she had a brief conversation with each of her children. It was personal yet spiritual at the same time. It was emotional. The room was filled with people who were crying.

It had gotten to the point where her words could only be heard as a whisper. I, however, was close enough to hear her clearly say that she forgave Mark Murcel. To me, her forgiveness meant that she had laid her differences to rest so she could finally get her peace. I believe she forgave her father a long time ago in her heart. I also believe that she wanted to give us an example so that we would forgive as well.

While we both stared into each other's eyes, I can remember her saying that I had done well and that God was going to bless me. After the conversations with all of us, she never spoke again. It was hurtful, but she was now at peace.

After a lavish funeral fit for a queen, I began reflecting on all the things that Mother had gone through and done in her life. I got a better understanding of God's plan from her. Mother robed herself with and maintained patience, obedience, and perseverance. That became a lifestyle for her during the good and bad times. I was reminded of the promise of long life, which I attributed to her patience and faithfulness. As I reflected on all the good seeds that she had sown in her life, I was also reminded of how she reaped in her season.

During the bad situations in her life, her rewards had always been greater because she had obeyed the Spirit who dwelled inside her. I am also reminded that she finally understood that her life was a race and that no matter what, she had to run until she completed it. So she persevered and endured until the end.

I AM FREE

A throbbing heart, a perplexed mind, and eyes blinded at sea
By two ships that set out sailing, en route to their destiny.
A voice clamored, "Strife," outside the ships. It demanded of me
By shouting, yelling, daring, and challenging my integrity.
Though hypnotized by the clamor, mine eyes fixated on the sea.
A whisper came from one ship, saying that it had a message for me.
I tried to move and get away because fear came naturally,
But I was enclosed in a war of voices, one making a louder plea.
Plainly but clearly, it stated, "A pattern, can't you see?"
Tears welled up and filled my eyes. My eyes slowly lifted from the sea
To a transformation of a newer truth and a newer clarity;
To a truth that would rule, reign, and make the clamor flee,
And to remind the lost once blinded, you are ready to go free.

www.ingramcontent.com/pod-product-compliance
Lightning Source LLC
LaVergne TN
LVHW041712060526
838201LV00043B/691